Lenny Hort HOW MANY STARS IN THE SKY?

Paintings by James E. Ransome

Tambourine Books/New York

Printed in the United States of America
Book design by Golda Laurens
First edition
10 9 8 7 6 5 4 3 2 1
The illustrations consist of oil paintings which were
scanner separated and reproduced in full color.

Library of Congress Cataloging in Publication Data
Hort, Lenny. How many stars in the sky? / by Lenny Hort ;
paintings by James E. Ransome.   p.   cm.
Summary: One night when Mama is away, Daddy and child
seek a good place to count the stars in the night sky.
ISBN 0-688-10103-8 (trade)—ISBN 0-688-10104-6 (lib.)
[1. Stars—Fiction. 2. Night—Fiction. 3. Father and child—
Fiction.] I. Ransome, James E., ill. II. Title.
PZ7.H7918Ho 1991 [E]—dc20   90-36044 CIP AC

For Aunt Vivian and in memory of Uncle Bill
L.C.H.

To Pops, my loving father
J. E.R.

How many stars in the sky?

Mama was away that night and I couldn't sleep. Mama knows all about the sun and stars. But she was away and I didn't want to wake Daddy. So I stared out the window asking myself: How many stars in the sky?

I could count so many just from my room. I leaned out the window and I could count even more. That was just gazing over the backyard. How many stars in the sky?

I went outside with a pad and pencil. I started to count. I filled up one whole page of the pad.

But there were lots of stars hidden behind the trees. The house blocked out even more. The streetlamp was so bright I couldn't see stars anywhere near it. How many stars in the sky?

I climbed high up into my treehouse. I started at the Big Dipper and counted in a great circle all around the sky. I filled up page after page of the pad.

But when I got back to the Dipper it wasn't where I remembered it. I must have been out so long that the stars had moved. Old ones had set. New ones had risen. How many stars in the sky?

I climbed down from the treehouse and there was Daddy. "I couldn't sleep," I said.

"I can't sleep either," he said. "Your mama won't be back till to-morrow."

I told him how I wanted to count all the stars in the sky.

"If your mama was here," Daddy said, "I bet she'd know. Maybe you and I can find someplace where it'll be easier to count them."

My dog hopped in the truck with us and we drove into town. The streets were quiet, but lots of streetlights were burning. We could see the bright city skyline in the distance.

Daddy and I counted twenty-five or twenty-six stars. He said he thought one of them was the planet Jupiter. "This isn't a good place to see stars," I said.

"It's not a bad place to count them, though," he said. "But it's still too hard. Let's go where it'll be really easy."

We drove into the city. The big clock by the tunnel said 2:45, but neither one of us felt like sleeping.

We parked by Mama's office. There was a department store with brightly lit displays in every window. There were streetlamps on every corner.

There were dazzling neon signs. Headlights flashed from a steady stream
of cars. Powerful searchlights beamed from the roofs of the skyscrapers.

And I couldn't see any stars at all. "I count exactly one," said Daddy.
"No, wait," he said, "it's an airplane."
"Maybe the stars just don't want to be counted," I said.

We drove back through the tunnel. I was tired, and I thought we were going home. But instead, Daddy drove us deep into the country.

There weren't any cars. There weren't any streetlights. There weren't any houses. Even the moon had set. And I knew we could never count all the stars.

No matter where I looked, new ones appeared every time I blinked my eyes. Daddy pointed up above and showed me the Milky Way. The stars were so thick I couldn't tell one from another.

We were much too tired to drive anymore, so we slept underneath

It was daylight when we woke. "Daddy," I said, "all those stars are always out there even when we can't see them, right?"

"Of course they are," he said.

"Can we try to count them again some time?" I asked.

"Any night you feel like it," he said, "you and me and Mama can all go out together."

I could hardly wait to see Mama and tell her about it. In a little while we'd all be back home. But now I was glad just to be standing there with Daddy, basking in the warmth of the one star we could see—

and that was the Sun.